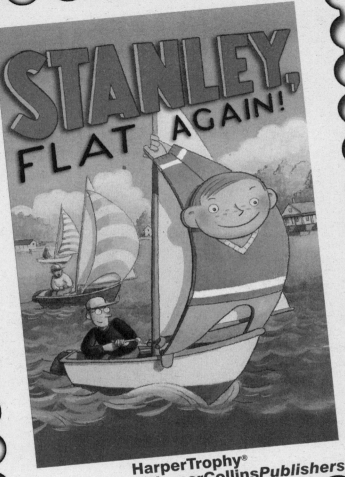

STANLEY, FLAT AGAIN!

HarperTrophy®
An Imprint of HarperCollinsPublishers

by Jeff Brown

Pictures by Scott Nash

Stanley, Flat Again!
Copyright © 2003 by Jeff Brown
Illustrations copyright © 2003 by Scott Nash

Library of Congress Cataloging-in-Publication Data
Brown, Jeff, 1926–
Stanley, Flat Again! / by Jeff Brown ; illustrated by Scott Nash.
    p.     cm.— (Flat Stanley)
    Summary: After Stanley Lambchop goes flat once again, he uses his flatness to help win a sail-
boat race and to rescue a classmate from a collapsed building.
    ISBN 0-06-009551-2 — ISBN 0-06-029826-X (lib. bdg.) — ISBN 0-06-442173-2 (pbk.)
    [1. Sailing—Fiction. 2. Humorous stories.] I. Nash, Scott, 1959– , ill. II. Title. III. Series.
PZ7.B81422 Sv 2003                                                                          2002003149
[Fic]—dc21                                                                                          CIP
                                                                                                    AC

❖
First Harper Trophy edition, 2004

Visit us on the World Wide Web!
www.harperchildrens.com
and www.flatstanleyproject.com

For Peter and Wendy,

Ozinger, Betsy, and Ash

# CONTENTS

DAILY SENTINEL
SUPER CHICKEN!
SWEDES
BREED
PEDDLING
POULTRY

FORCE

# A MORNING SURPRISE

Mrs. Lambchop was making breakfast. Mr. Lambchop, at the kitchen table, helped by reading bits from the morning paper.

"Here's an odd one, Harriet," he said. "There's a chicken in Sweden that rides a bike."

"So do I, George," said Mrs. Lambchop, not really listening.

"Listen to this. 'Merker Building emptied. To be collapsed next week.' Imagine! Eight floors!"

"Poor thing!" Mrs. Lambchop set out plates. "Boys!" she called. "Breakfast is ready!"

Her glance fell upon a row of photographs

on the wall above the sink. There was a smiling Stanley, only half an inch thick, his big bulletin board having fallen from the bedroom wall to rest upon him overnight. Next came reminders of the many family adventures that had come after Stanley's younger brother,

Arthur, had cleverly blown him round again with a bicycle pump. There were the brothers with Prince Haraz, the young genie who had granted wishes for them all after being accidentally summoned by Stanley from a lamp. There was the entire family with Santa Claus and his daughter, Sarah, taken during a Christmas visit to the North Pole. There was the family again in Washington, D.C., in the office of the President of the United States, who had asked them to undertake a secret mission into outer space. The last picture showed Arthur standing beside a balloon on which Mrs. Lambchop had painted a picture of Stanley's face. The balloon, its string in fact held by Stanley, had been a valuable guide to his presence, since he was invisible at the time. "Boys!" she called again. "Breakfast!"

In their bedroom, Stanley and Arthur had finished dressing.

While Stanley filled his backpack, Arthur bounced a tennis ball. "Let's go," he said. "Here! Catch!"

Stanley had just reached for a book on the shelf by his bed. The ball struck his back as he turned, and he banged his shoulder on a corner of the shelf.

"Ouch!"

"Sorry," Arthur said. "But let's go, okay? You know how long— STANLEY!"

"Why are you shouting?" Stanley adjusted his pack. "C'mon! I'm so hungry—" He paused. "Oh, boy! Arthur, do you see?"

"I do, actually." Arthur swallowed hard.

"You're, you know . . . Flat."

The brothers stared at each other.

"The pump?" Stanley said. "It might work again."

Arthur fetched the bicycle pump from their toy chest, and Stanley lay on his bed with the hose end in his mouth.

Arthur gave a long, steady, pump.

Stanley made a face. "That hurts!"

Arthur pumped again, and Stanley snatched the hose from his mouth. "Owww! That really hurts! It wasn't like that before. We'd better stop."

"Now what?" Arthur said. "We can't just hide in here forever, you know."

Mrs. Lambchop's call came again. "Boys! Please come!"

"Do me a favor," Stanley said. "You tell them. Sort of get them ready, okay?"

"Okay," said Arthur, and went to tell.

Arthur stood in the kitchen doorway. "Hey, guess what?" he said.

"Hay is for horses, dear," said Mrs. Lambchop. "Good morning! Breakfast is ready."

"Good morning, Arthur," Mr. Lambchop said from behind his newspaper. "Where's Stanley?"

"Guess what?" Arthur said again.

Mrs. Lambchop sighed. "Oh, all right! I can't guess. Tell."

"Stanley's flat again," said Arthur.

Mr. Lambchop put down his paper.

Mrs. Lambchop closed her eyes. "Flat again? Is that what you said?"

"Yes," said Arthur.

"It's true." Stanley stood now beside Arthur in the doorway. "Just look."

"Good grief!" said Mr. Lambchop. "I can't believe that bulletin board—"

"It didn't fall on me this time," Stanley said. "I just got flat. Arthur tried to pump me

up, like before, but it hurt too much."

"Oh, Stanley!" Mrs. Lambchop ran to kiss him. "How do you feel now?"

"Fine, actually," Stanley said. "Just surprised. Can I go to school?"

Mrs. Lambchop thought for a moment. "Very well. Eat your breakfast. After school we'll hear what Dr. Dan has to say."

# DR. DAN

"Ah, Mr. and Mrs. Lambchop! And the boys!" said Dr. Dan as they entered his office. "How nice to—"

His eyes widened. "Good heavens, Stanley! Mr. Lambchop, you really must do something about that bulletin board!"

"It is still firmly in place, Dr. Dan," Mrs. Lambchop said. "We are at a loss to account for this attack of flatness."

"Hmmm." Dr. Dan thought for a moment. "Is there, perhaps, a family history of flatness?"

"No," Mr. Lambchop said. "We'd remember that."

"We got dressed for school," Stanley explained. "We didn't even have breakfast. And all of a sudden, I got flat."

Dr. Dan frowned. "Nothing happened? Nothing at all?"

"Well, Arthur hit me with a tennis ball," Stanley said. "And then I banged my shoulder on—"

"Aha!" Jumping up, Dr. Dan took a large book from the case behind his desk and began turning pages. "This is Dr. Franz

Gemeister's excellent *Difficult and Peculiar Cases*. Just let me find . . . Here it is! 'Flatness, page two seventeen!'"

He read aloud. "'Sudden flatness . . . extremely rare . . . minimal documentation . . . hearsay reports . . .' Ah, here it is! Dates back to the fifth century! 'During battle, Mongo the Fierce, an aide to Attila the Hun, was struck twice, simultaneously, from behind, and at once became no thicker than his shield. He became known as Mongo the Plate, and lived to old age without regaining his original girth.'"

Dr. Dan closed the book. "As I suspected! The OBP."

"Beg pardon?" said Mrs. Lambchop.

"The OBP. Osteal Balance Point," Dr. Dan explained. "A little-known anatomical feature. The human body, of course, is a complex miracle, its skeleton a delicate framework of supports and balances. The Osteal Balance Point may occur almost anywhere in the upper torso. It is vulnerable only to the application of simultaneous pressures at two points which vary depending on the age and particular 'design,' let us say, of the individual involved. In my opinion, the pressures created by the tennis ball and the shelf corner affected Stanley's OBP, thereby turning him flat."

For a moment, everyone was silent.

"The first time Stanley went flat, you were greatly puzzled by his condition," Mr. Lambchop said at last. "Now you seem remarkably well informed."

"I read up on it," said Dr. Dan.

Mrs. Lambchop sighed. "Perhaps we should seek a second opinion. Who is the world's leading authority on the OBP?"

"That would be me," said Dr. Dan.

"I see. . . . Well, we've taken enough of your time." Mr. Lambchop rose, motioning his family to follow. "Thank you, Dr. Dan."

At the door, Mrs. Lambchop turned. "Perhaps if we found the, you know, the OBP, we could make Stanley—"

"No, no!" said Dr. Dan. "It would be

dangerous to put the lad through such a skeletal strain again! And finding the OBP? Not very likely, I'm afraid."

Arthur had an idea. "I know! If we all got sticks and hit Stanley all over at the same time, and kept doing it, then—"

"That will do, Arthur," Mr. Lambchop said, and led his family out.

# STANLEY
# SAILS

Early the next Sunday morning, Mr. Lambchop had a call from an old college friend, Ralph Jones.

"Just wanted to remind you, George, that Stanley and I have a date to go sailing today," he said.

"He's looking forward to it, Ralph." Mr. Lambchop hesitated. "I should mention, perhaps, that Stanley has gone flat again."

Mr. Jones sighed. "I thought he'd got over that. Well, I'll pick him up at ten."

Later that morning, driving with Stanley to his sailing club on the seashore, Mr. Jones inquired about a foreign visitor he had once met with the Lambchops. "A prince, yes? He around these days?"

Stanley knew he meant the young genie, Prince Haraz, but it would be difficult to explain not only the genie part, but also that Haraz had returned to the genie kingdom from which he had come.

"No," Stanley said. "He went home, actually."

"Too bad." Mr. Jones was famous for his amazing memory. "Haraz, as I recall.

Prince Fawzi Mustafa Aslan Mirza Malek Namerd Haraz?"

"Right," said Stanley.

In the harbor of the sailing club, Mr. Jones prepared his boat, *Lovebug*, and explained it to Stanley. "This big sail here is the mainsail, and that's the rudder back there, for steering. In this zip bag is another sail, called a spinnaker. We'll use that one for extra speed when we're running before the wind. See that boat way out there, how its spinnaker is puffing out front?"

Stanley laughed. The spinnaker looked like an open umbrella lying on its side.

"See over there," Mr. Jones went on, "between the committee boat, with the judges on it, and the red buoy? That's the starting line. The race ends back there too. First boat to cross that line wins!"

He cast off the mooring line, and the mainsail filled. *Lovebug* headed out to join the other boats.

Mr. Jones pointed. "There! That's Jasper Green's boat, *Windswept*. He's the one I want especially to beat!"

"Why? Are you mad at him?" Stanley asked.

"He was very rude to me once. But never mind. Let's just make sure we win!"

Behind the start line, they found themselves beside *Windswept*. Jasper Green gave a friendly wave, but Ralph Jones ignored him.

"You're always in a bad mood with me, Ralph," Mr. Green said. "Why? I don't— Here we go!"

A pistol shot had signaled the start of the race. *Lovebug* and *Windswept* and the other racers glided across the start line behind the motor-powered committee boat, which led them along a course marked by buoys with bright green streamers.

Stanley sat back, enjoying himself. The sun was bright, the breeze fresh against his face, the sky clear and blue, the water a beautiful slate color. There were boats on both sides of them, boats ahead, boats behind. How pretty they were, their white sails making cheerful crackling sounds as they billowed in the wind!

Along the shore, people waved from the porches of houses, their voices carrying faintly on the wind. "Way to go! . . . Looking good, sailors! . . . Looking flat, one of them!" Stanley waved back, knowing that the teasing was kindly meant.

*Lovebug* passed other boats, but there were many more still ahead. And now they were almost abreast of *Windswept*.

Stanley saw that Jasper Green had hoisted his spinnaker, and that other boats had too.

"I've got you beat, Ralph!" Jasper Green shouted.

"We'll just round this point, Stanley! Then— Now!" exclaimed Ralph Jones. "Let's show Jasper what running before the wind really means!"

He attached his spinnaker to a halyard and ran it up the mast. *Who-o-oosh!* The spinnaker billowed out, and Stanley felt *Lovebug* surge forward, as if pushed by an invisible hand.

"Here we go!" shouted Ralph Jones.

They passed five more boats, three more, then *Windswept*! They were ahead of everyone now, and the finish line lay ahead!

"We're going to win!" Stanley shouted.

"Yes!" Ralph Jones shouted back. "Just wait till Jasper—"

*R-i-i-i-p!*

The sound came from above. Looking up, they saw that the top of the spinnaker had torn.

*R-i-i-i-i-i-p!*

The rip streaked downward, and now the spinnaker, torn all the way down, flapped uselessly in the wind. *Lovebug* slowed.

"Drat!" Mr. Jones did his best with the mainsail. "Drat, drat, drat!"

*Windswept* came up behind them. "Tough luck!" called Jasper Green. "Ha, ha!"

"Drat!" Mr. Jones sighed. "Nothing we can do, Stanley. Unless— This may be crazy, but . . . Stanley, perhaps you could be our spinnaker?"

"What?" Stanley shouted. "How?"

"Good question," said Mr. Jones. "Let's see . . . First, go take hold of the mast. That's it. Now maybe—"

"Excuse me," Stanley said. "But did you ever do this before?"

"Stanley, *nobody* ever did this before." Mr. Jones took a deep breath. "Okay. Now twist around to face forward, and grab the mast behind you above your head!"

Stanley did as he was told, planting his feet on the sides of the boat to hold him in place. The wind pressed him from behind, driving *Lovebug* toward the finish line.

"Yes! Chest forward! Butt back!" shouted

Mr. Jones. "Best spinnaker I ever had!" In a moment they had passed *Windswept*, and Stanley could not help laughing at the surprise on Jasper Green's face.

And then they were across the finish line! *Lovebug* had won!

Back in the clubhouse, Jasper Green would not admit that he had lost. A flat person used as a sail? He had never seen *that* before, he said, and went to the race committee office to complain. But he returned shortly to report that *Lovebug* had indeed won. The committee had advised him, he said, that there was no rule against a crew member allowing the wind to blow against him.

"Great sailing, Ralph!" he said. "I thought

it was my race, I really did!"

"Thank you, Jasper," Mr. Jones said, but Stanley noticed that he did not smile.

Jasper Green noticed too. "Ralph, you're still mad at me," he said. "But *why*?"

"You spilled coffee on my white pants, Jasper," said Ralph Jones. "And you just laughed when I jumped up."

"What?" Jasper Green seemed greatly surprised. "I don't remember— Where? When?"

"We were having lunch," said Mr. Jones. "At the old Vandercook Hotel."

"The Vandercook? It closed down twenty years ago!" Mr. Green slapped his forehead. "I *do* remember! That lunch was twenty years ago, Ralph!"

"Twenty-one, actually."

"All right, all right!" said Mr. Green. "I apologize, for heaven's sake!"

Ralph Jones smiled warmly. "Perfectly all right, Jasper," he said. "Don't give it another thought."

# BACK TO
# SCHOOL

Stanley was pleased that his classmates, who still remembered his previous flatness, made no great fuss about it now. Mostly they expressed only cheerful interest. "Feeling okay, Stan?" they said, and "Lookin' sharp, man! Sharp, see? Get the joke?" Only mean Emma Weeks was unpleasant. "Huh! Mr. Show-off again!" Emma said one day, but

Stanley pretended not to hear.

He had been back at school for a week when a newspaper, learning of this unusually shaped student, sent a photographer to investigate. He found Stanley watching a practice on the soccer field.

"Flash Tobin," he said. "From the *Daily Sentinel*. You're the flat kid, right?"

Stanley thought he must be joking. "How did you know?" he said, joking back.

"How did I—" The photographer laughed. "Oh, I get it! Can I take your picture, kid? Right here by the goal posts?"

Stanley nodded, and Flash Tobin took his picture. "I heard there was a flat kid here before," he said. "Helped catch sneak thieves at the Famous Museum of Art. But that kid, I heard he got round again."

"It was me," Stanley told him.

"You go back and forth, huh?" The photographer was impressed. "Okay, get round
now. I'd like a shot of that too."

"I can't just do it when I want," Stanley
explained. "The first time, my brother had to
blow me up. With a bicycle pump."

"Make a great picture!" Flash Tobin shook

his head. "Well, we'll just go with flat."

Stanley's picture was in the *Daily Sentinel* the next morning, and Arthur could not help showing his jealousy. Stanley was always getting his picture in the paper, he said. Didn't they see how interesting it would be to have a picture of his brother?

There was a soccer team practice that afternoon, and the day was windy. It was worrisome, the coach said, the way Stanley got blown about. Perhaps, for the sake of the team, he should switch to an indoor sport.

Stanley loved soccer, and the more he thought about what the coach had said, the sadder he felt.

Miss Elliott, his homeroom teacher, noticed that he was not his usual cheerful self. "Mr. Redfield, the new guidance counselor, is said to be very helpful to troubled students," she told him. "I will ask him to find time for you."

Miss Elliott spoke to him again after lunch. "Such good luck, Stanley! Mr. Redfield will see you right after school today!"

"Come in, Stanley. Sit right there!" Mr. Redfield pointed to a comfortable chair.

Stanley sat, and Mr. Redfield leaned back behind his desk. "Now then. . . . You do understand that anything you say here is completely confidential? I won't tell anybody."

Stanley wondered what he could say that would interest anybody else.

"Miss Elliott tells me you seem troubled."
Mr. Redfield lowered his voice. "What's
wrong?"

"I'm not sure, actually," Stanley said.

Mr. Redfield picked up a pad and a pen.
"Speak freely. Whatever comes into your
head. Anything special happen lately?"

"Well, I got flat," Stanley said.

Mr. Redfield made a note on his pad. "I do
see that, yes. How did that make you feel?"

Stanley thought for a moment. "Flat."

"I see." Mr. Redfield nodded. "This flatness, it's come upon you before, I'm told. Is it
possible that somehow, without even admit-
ting it to yourself, you wanted it to happen
again?"

"No way!" Stanley said firmly. "The first

time, it was kind of fun for a while. Flying like a kite, and being mailed to California, things like that. But then I got, you know, tired of it. And now I might get put off the soccer team."

Mr. Redfield nodded again. "You take no pleasure now in your unusual shape?"

Stanley thought for a moment. "Well, sometimes." He told about being a sail, and helping Ralph Jones win a race.

Mr. Redfield made another note. "I see. This dream of being a sail, have you dreamed it before?"

Stanley stared at him. "It wasn't a . . . It really happened! I'm just tired of being different, I guess."

Mr. Redfield pressed his fingertips together.

"Different? How do you feel different, would you say?"

Stanley wondered how Mr. Redfield could be a good guidance counselor if he had both terrible eyesight and a terrible memory.

"Well, I'm the only one in my class who's flat," he said. "The whole school, actually."

"Interesting." Mr. Redfield made another note and glanced at his watch. "I'm afraid our time is up, Stanley. Would you like to see me again? Just let Miss Elliott know."

"Okay," Stanley said politely, but he didn't think he would.

# WHY ME?

Stanley had looked sad all evening, Arthur thought. At bedtime, as they lay waiting for Mr. and Mrs. Lambchop to come say good night, he wondered how to cheer his brother up.

It was raining hard, and he remembered suddenly the rainy evening that Stanley had snacked on raisins, and by morning had become invisible. A little-known conse-quence, Dr. Dan had explained, of eating fruit during bad weather.

"Hear the rain, Stanley?" he said. "Better not eat any fruit."

"Ha, ha, ha." Stanley sounded cross. "Just leave me alone, okay?"

"Stanley's in a terrible mood," Arthur told Mr. and Mrs. Lambchop when they came in. "He won't even talk to me."

"What's wrong, my boy?" Mr Lambchop asked.

"Nothing." Stanley put his pillow over his head.

"If my picture was in the newspaper practically every day, I'd be happy," Arthur said. "I mean, why—"

Mrs. Lambchop hushed him. "Stanley, dear? What is troubling you?"

"Nothing. Nothing," Stanley said from under the pillow, and sat up. "But why me? Why am I always getting flat, or invisible or something? Why can't it just once be someone else?"

"I wouldn't mind, actually," Arthur said. "Just for a while. I—"

"Hush, Arthur!" Mrs. Lambchop put out the overhead light, lit a corner lamp, and sat by Stanley on his bed. Mr. Lambchop sat with Arthur. The gentle patter of the rain against the windows, the glow of the little lamp, made the bedroom cozy indeed.

"I do see what you mean, Stanley," Mr. Lambchop said at last. "Why do these things happen to you? Your mother and I don't know the answer either. But things often happen without there seeming to be a reason, and then something else happens, and suddenly the first thing seems to have had a purpose after all."

"Well put, George!" Mrs. Lambchop squeezed Stanley's hand. "What we do know, Stanley dear, is that we're very proud of you, and love you very much. And we understand about the flatness, and all the other unexpected happenings, how upsetting it must be."

"It sure is!" said Stanley. "How would you like never knowing when you might get flat?

Or invisible? Maybe someday I'll wake up ten feet tall or one inch short, or with green hair, or a tail or something!"

"I know. . . ." Mrs. Lambchop said softly, and Mr. Lambchop came and patted Stanley's shoulder. Then they kissed both boys, switched off the lamp, and went out.

Arthur spoke into the darkened room. "Stanley?"

"I'm trying to sleep," said Stanley. "What?"

"I was just thinking," Arthur said. "If you got invisible, and then you got flat, how would they know?"

"Huh? I don't—" Stanley laughed. "Oh, I get it! About the flatness. Good one, Arthur."

Arthur laughed too.

"Quiet, please," said Stanley. "I'm trying to sleep."

"Okay," Arthur said, but he chuckled several times before he fell asleep.

# EMMA

Mr. Lambchop came home early the next afternoon, full of excitement.

"Guess what?" he said. "The old Merker Department Store downtown? Eight floors, all emptied out, waiting to be torn down? Well, last night most of it fell down by itself!" He switched on the TV. "News time! Let's get the latest!"

". . . more on the Merker building collapse!" a newscaster was saying. "It's just a mountain of rubble now, folks! Three workmen have been treated for minor bruises, but no other injuries are reported. The public is requested to avoid the area until—"

A young woman ran on, handed him a slip of paper, and ran off again.

"Hold on! This just in!" The newscaster read from the slip. "Wow! A little girl is trapped under all that wreckage! Emma Weeks, daughter of local businessman Oswald Weeks!"

"Emma Weeks!" Stanley exclaimed. "She's in my class! No wonder she wasn't at school today!"

"Emma's not hurt, it appears," the newscaster continued. "Firemen called to the scene can hear her calling up through chinks in the wreckage, demanding food and water! But Fire Chief Johnson has forbidden any rescue efforts! Any disturbance, any shifting of the wreckage, he says, might bring the rest of the building crashing down! Now, here's Tom Miller!"

The TV screen showed a reporter with a microphone standing by the wrecked building.

"Emma Weeks!" shouted the reporter, holding his microphone up to a crack. "Do you hear me? Are you all right?"

Emma's voice was faint but clear. "Oh, sure! I'm just great! I hope a building falls

on me every day, you know? C'mon, get me out of here!"

Mrs. Lambchop sighed. "Such an unfortunate tone! She is under great strain, of course."

"Emma's always like that," Stanley said.

Half an hour later, while Mrs. Lambchop was preparing supper, a siren sounded outside, then died away. Opening the front door, Mr. Lambchop saw a Fire Department car at the curb. On the doorstep stood Fire Chief Johnson and a very worried-looking man and woman.

"Mr. Lambchop?" said Chief Johnson. "I'll get right to the point, sir. I reckon you heard about little Emma Weeks, trapped in the Merker wreck? Well, Mr. and Mrs. Weeks here, and me, we'd like a word with you folks."

"Of course!" Mr. Lambchop led the visitors into the house and introduced them to his family.

"Oh, Mrs. Weeks!" Mrs. Lambchop cried. "Your poor daughter! You must be dreadfully worried!"

"We are indeed!" said Mr. Weeks. "But Chief Johnson thinks your Stanley might be able to save Emma!"

"Who, me?" and "Who, Stanley?" said Stanley and Arthur.

Chief Johnson explained. "Problem is that if a policeman, or one of my firemen, tries to dig his way in to Emma, the whole rest of the building could crash down on 'em! Too bad we don't have a flat fireman, I was thinking. Flat fella could squeeze through all those narrow openings we know are there, 'cause we hear Emma when she calls. Then I recollected the newspaper story, with a picture of Stanley here. Hit me right away! *That* boy could maybe wiggle in to Emma!"

For a moment, everyone was silent. Then Mrs. Lambchop shook her head.

"It sounds terribly dangerous," she said. "I'm sorry, but I must say no."

"It is a tad risky, ma'am," said Chief Johnson. "But we've got to remember the boy is already flat."

Mrs. Weeks sobbed. "Oh, poor Emma! How are we to save her?"

Mrs. Lambchop bit her lip.

Stanley remembered something. "I was just thinking." He turned to Mr. Lambchop.

"The other night? When I got mad about all the crazy things that keep happening to me? Remember what you said? You said that sometime things happen that nobody can see a reason for, and then afterwards some other thing happens, and all of a sudden it seems like the first thing had a reason after all. Well, I was just thinking that me getting flat again was one crazy thing, and that maybe Emma getting stuck where I'm the only one who can try to save her, that might be the second thing."

Mr. Lambchop nodded, and took Mrs.

Lambchop's hand. "We should be very proud of our son, Harriet."

Mrs. Lambchop thought for a moment. "Stanley," she said at last. "Will you be very, very, careful not to let that enormous building fall on you?"

"Okay. Sure," Stanley said.

Mrs. Lambchop turned to Mr. and Mrs. Weeks. "We will allow Stanley to help," she said. "He will do his best for Emma."

"Fine boy we got here! Brave as a lion!" shouted Chief Johnson. "Now listen up, folks! Mrs. Lambchop, you help me get things ready! Then Stanley can go right in after Emma! Got that? Everybody meet us at the Merker Building, thirty minutes from now!"

# WHERE ARE YOU, EMMA?

In the late afternoon sunlight, at the remains of the old Merker building, the Lambchops and the Weekses watched Chief Johnson prepare Stanley for his rescue attempt. Flash Tobin, the *Daily Sentinel* photographer, was there too, taking pictures.

Mrs. Lambchop had supplied two slices of bread and cheese, each wrapped in plastic, and her grandfather's flat silver cigarette case filled with grape soda. Chief Johnson taped the bread and cheese packets to Stanley's arms and legs, the cigarette case to his chest, and gave him a small, flat flashlight.

Then he led Stanley up to a tall crack in the wreckage. "Emma!" he shouted. "Fella's coming to help you! When he calls your name, you holler back 'Here!' so he knows which way to go. Got that?"

Emma's voice came faintly. "Yeah, yeah! Hurry up! I'm starving!"

Chief Johnson shook Stanley's hand. "Good luck, son!"

The evening sunlight glowed warmly on the red bricks of the fallen building as Stanley stepped close to the crack. Mrs.

Lambchop waved to him, and Stanley waved back. How handsome he is, she thought. How brave, how tall, how flat!

Stanley took two steps forward and disappeared sideways through the crack. A moment later they heard his shout. "Hey! It's really dark in here!"

"Hay is for horses, Stanley!" Mrs. Lambchop called back. "Oh, never mind! Good luck, dear!"

This was a dark greater than any he had ever known. Stanley could almost feel the blackness on his skin. He clicked on his flashlight and edged forward without difficulty, but then the crack narrowed, slowing him. The bread slice on his left leg had scraped something, loosening the tape that held it. Pressing the tape back into place, he wiggled forward until he came to what seemed a dead end, but a little swing of the flashlight showed cracks branching right and left.

"Emma?" he called.

"Here!"

Her voice came from the right, so he moved along that branch. "Emma?"

"Yeah, yeah! What?"

"When I say your name, you're supposed to say 'Here!'"

"I already did that!"

He followed another crack to the left. "Emma?"

There was no answer. Stanley managed a few more feet and then, quite suddenly, the crack widened. He called again. "Emma?"

"Bananas!"

"Keep talking," he shouted. "I need to hear you!"

"Bananas! Here! Blah, blah! Whatever! Hey, I can see your light!"

And there she was. The crack had widened to become a small cave, at the back of which sat Emma. Her jeans and shirt were smudged with dirt, but it was most surely Emma, squinting against the brightness of his light.

"You!" she exclaimed. "From school! The flattie!"

Don't lose your temper, Stanley told himself. "I was the only one they thought could get in here. How are you doing, Emma?"

Emma rolled her eyes. "Oh, just great! A

whole building falls on me, and they send in a flattie! And now I'm starving to death!"

Stanley untaped the slices of bread and cheese, and handed them over.

"Cheese, huh?" Emma put her sandwich together and took a bite. "I hate cheese. Got anything to drink, flattie?"

"Please don't call me flattie. Here." He held out the silver cigarette case.

Emma rolled her eyes again. "I'm not allowed to smoke."

"It's soda."

She opened the cigarette case and sipped. "Blaahh! I hate grape!"

Chief Johnson's voice rose from a hole in the wall behind her. "Stanley? You there yet?"

Emma jerked a thumb at the hole. "It's for you, flattie."

"I'm here, Chief!" Stanley called. "Emma's okay."

He heard cheering, and then the Chief's voice came again. "See a way out, Stan?"

"I haven't had a chance to look around yet. Emma's eating."

"We'll wait. Over and out, Stan!"

"You too!" Stanley called.

He waited until Emma had finished her sandwich. "Emma, how did you get into this mess? What made you come in here?"

"I just came over to look," Emma said. "And they had all these signs! 'Danger! Keep out!' All over the place, even behind in the parking lot. 'Keep out! Danger! Danger!' I

really hate that, you know? So there was this door, and it was open, so I went in." She finished the grape soda. "Okay, let's go."

"Not the way I came in," Stanley said. "I could just barely squeeze through. And we have to be careful, because—"

"I know!" Emma interrupted. "Chief whats-hisname kept telling me: 'Don't move around! The whole rest of the building might crash down!' So am I supposed to live down here forever?"

"This door you came through," Stanley said. "How far did you come to find this sort of cave we're in?"

"Who said anything about far? I just got inside, and there were these crashing noises, and the whole building was shaking, and I fell down right here! The crashing went on forever! I thought I was going to die!"

"Calm down." An idea came into Stanley's head. "Just where was this door? Do you remember?"

"Over there somewhere." Emma pointed into the darkness of a corner behind her.

Stanley swung his light, but saw only what seemed to be a solid wall of splintered boards, rock, and brick.

Emma pointed a bit left, then right. "Maybe there . . . I don't know! Was I supposed to take pictures or something? What difference does it make?"

"We might be just a little bit inside that door," Stanley said. "And what we want is to be just outside of it."

Moving closer to the corner, he saw that a jagged piece of wood protruded at waist level. It came out easily when he tugged, followed by loose dirt.

Emma stood beside him. "Why are you making this mess?"

He poked in the hole with the stick. "Maybe I'll find—"

Dirt cascaded from the wall, covering his shoes. He saw light now, not just the little circle from his flashlight, but daylight! Unmistakably daylight!

"Oooohhhh!" said Emma.

Stanley made the hole still larger, and they saw that a door lay on its side across the bottom of the hole, wreckage limiting the opening on both sides. But it was big enough! They would be able to wiggle through! He ran back to the wall from which Chief Johnson's voice had come.

"We're on our way out!" he shouted. "We'll be in back, in the courtyard!"

"Got it!" came the Chief's voice. "Great work!"

Stanley turned to Emma. "Let's go!"

"I'll get all dirty, silly," Emma said. "Maybe we could just—"

"Come ON!"

"Don't yell!" Emma said, but she crawled quickly through the hole with Stanley right behind her.

# HERO!

There was much rejoicing in the courtyard.
Mrs. Lambchop kissed Stanley and Arthur.
Mrs. Weeks kissed Emma, and then everyone
else, even Flash Tobin, who had arrived to
take pictures. Mr. Lambchop shook hands
with Mr. Weeks and Chief Johnson, who
announced several times that Stanley was a
great hero.

Flash Tobin took a group picture of all the Lambchops. "Need one more," he said. "Emma, just you and Stanley. Your hero, right? Saved your life!"

"I could have got out by myself," Emma said. "I just didn't know exactly where the door was." But she went to stand by Stanley.

"Smile!" Flash Tobin took the picture. "Yes, that's good!" He gave Stanley a cheerful slap on the back, just as Emma's elbow jabbed hard into Stanley's ribs.

"Owww!" Stanley yelled.

Emma grinned. "That's for you, Mr. Hero!"

"Are you crazy? What—" Stanley stopped. Everybody was staring at him. He felt peculiar, as if— Yes! He was getting round again!

"Wow!" Emma said. "How do you do that?"

"Hooray for you, dear!" shouted Mrs. Lambchop, and more cries rose from the others in the courtyard. "Do you see what I see? . . . He's blowing up! . . . Are we crazy or what?"

Flash Tobin aimed his camera again. "Hold it, kid!"

But he was too late. Before him now stood a smiling Stanley Lambchop, shaped like a regular boy!

Mr. Lambchop ran to hug him, and everyone else applauded.

"Been thirty years with the Fire

Department, and never saw anything like that!" said Chief Johnson. "Wouldn't have missed it!"

"I'm really glad," Stanley said. "But what made it happen?"

"What Dr. Dan said!" shouted Arthur. "Remember? The Osteo-posteo-whatever!"

"The OBP! The Osteal Balance Point." Mr. Lambchop smiled. "Yes! The slap on the back from Flash Tobin, and the poke from Emma! That did it!"

A board fell from the tilting roof of the Merker Building, landing in a corner of the courtyard.

"Let's go, folks," said Chief Johnson. "We're not safe here!"

A moment later, back out in the street,

there was more hugging and kissing and saying good night. Suddenly, behind them, there were great creaking and grinding sounds. Turning, they watched what was left of the Merker building come crashing down.

Emma spoke first. "Oh, boy," she said softly. "Wow!"

Mrs. Weeks caught her eye, and gave a little nod toward Stanley.

Emma looked puzzled. "Huh? . . . Oh, yeah!" She turned to Stanley. "I guess maybe you, you know, saved my life. Whatever." She kissed his cheek. "Thank you very much, Stanley Lambchop."

"It's okay," Stanley said, quite red in the face. "You're welcome."

Everyone went home.

# FAME!

At bedtime the next evening, the Lambchops read again the *Daily Sentinel* they had enjoyed so much at breakfast that morning.

The front page headline read: RUDE GIRL SAVED! FLAT RESCUER REGAINS SHAPE! There were also two Flash Tobin photographs—the Lambchop family picture and the one of Stanley and Emma taken just before she

HERO'S
BROTHER

poked him in the ribs. Arthur was particularly pleased with the family picture.

"Finally!" he said. "Not just Stanley! People could have been wondering if he had a brother, you know? Can I have this one?"

"You may," said Mrs. Lambchop. "I want the one of Stanley with Emma, for my kitchen wall."

"I don't care about pictures," Stanley said. "I just hope I never go back to being flat."

Mrs. Lambchop patted his hand. "I told Dr. Dan of your recovery, dear. He thinks it most unlikely the flatness will occur again."

"Yay!" said Stanley.

Arthur cut the family picture out of the paper, and used a red pencil to draw an arrow, pointing up at him, in the white space at the

bottom. Under the arrow, he wrote, *Hero's Brother*. Then he taped the picture to the wall above his bed.

Soon all the Lambchops were asleep.

## Send Flat Stanley on a whole new adventure!

After Stanley Lambchop is flattened by a bulletin board in *Flat Stanley*, he is able to travel through the mail in an envelope and visit his friend in California. With this post-card, you can send your own Flat Stanley on a new adventure through the mail!

To learn more about the many people sending Flat Stanley around the world, log on to **www.flatstanleyproject.com** or visit **www.harperchildrens.com**